This
Ladybird book
belongs to

....

To Megan,
for always hanging
in there
C.G.

For my family
M.H.

LADYBIRD BOOKS

UK | USA | Canada | Ireland | Australia | India | New Zealand | South Africa

Ladybird Books is part of the Penguin Random House group of companies

whose addresses can be found at global.penguinrandomhouse.com.

www.penguin.co.uk   www.puffin.co.uk   www.ladybird.co.uk

Penguin
Random House
UK

First published 2019

001

Written by Charlie Green. Text copyright © Ladybird Books Ltd, 2019

Illustrations copyright © Matt Hunt, 2019

Moral rights asserted

Printed in Italy

A CIP catalogue record for this book is available from the British Library

ISBN: 978–0–241–39517–2

All correspondence to:

Ladybird Books, Penguin Random House Children's

80 Strand, London WC2R 0RL

CHOOSE SLOTHS

Written by
Charlie Green

Illustrated by
Matt Hunt

Which sloth would you choose to organize your birthday party?

This is going to be totally **awesome.**

Charlie

Amy

I love party planning! I'll be ready in a year.

Ava

What would **YOU** choose to eat at your party?

Freddie

Tia

Which sloth would you choose as your yoga buddy?
Rianna
Josh
Do you want to hang out with me?
Can YOU do any yoga poses?
Jasmine

Which sloth would you choose to be stranded on a desert island with?

Which sloth would you choose to enter a diving competition with?

I can do three somersaults in a row!

Tom

I'm just warming up, guys. I'll see you down there in a week.

Mia

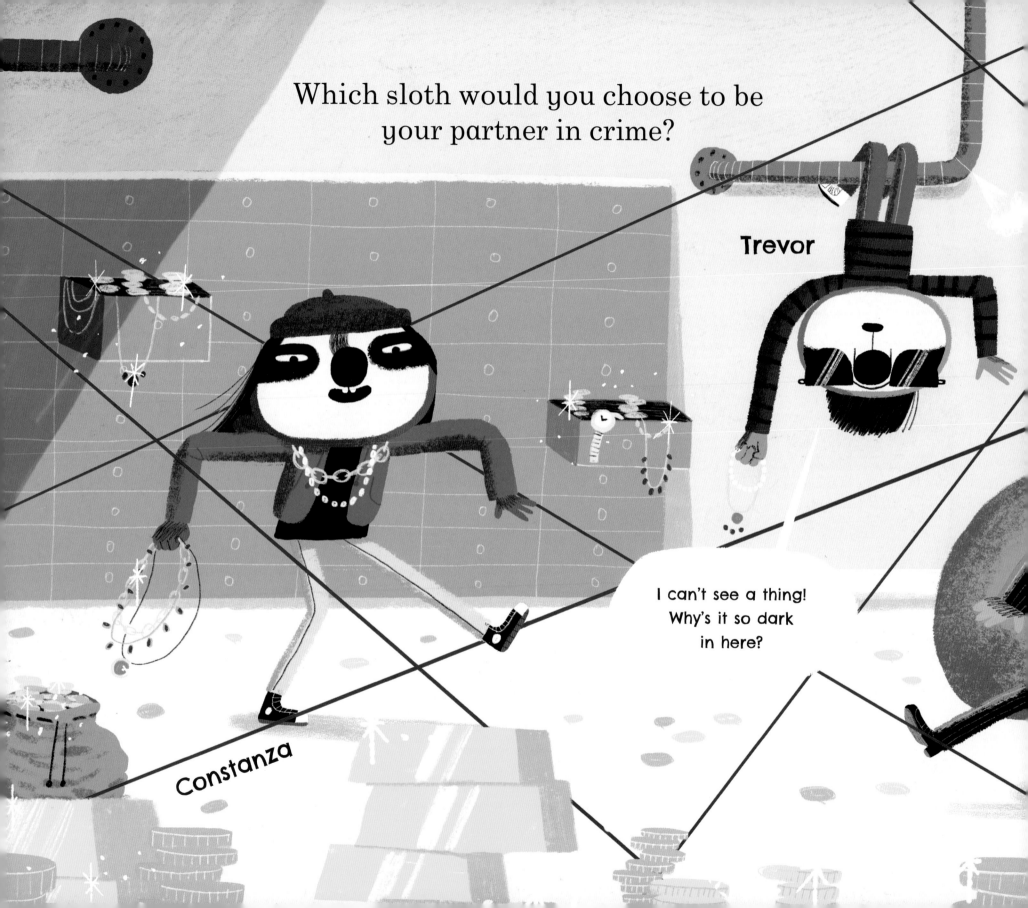

Which sloth would you choose to bounce around on a trampoline with?

Which sloth would you choose to go to the cinema with?

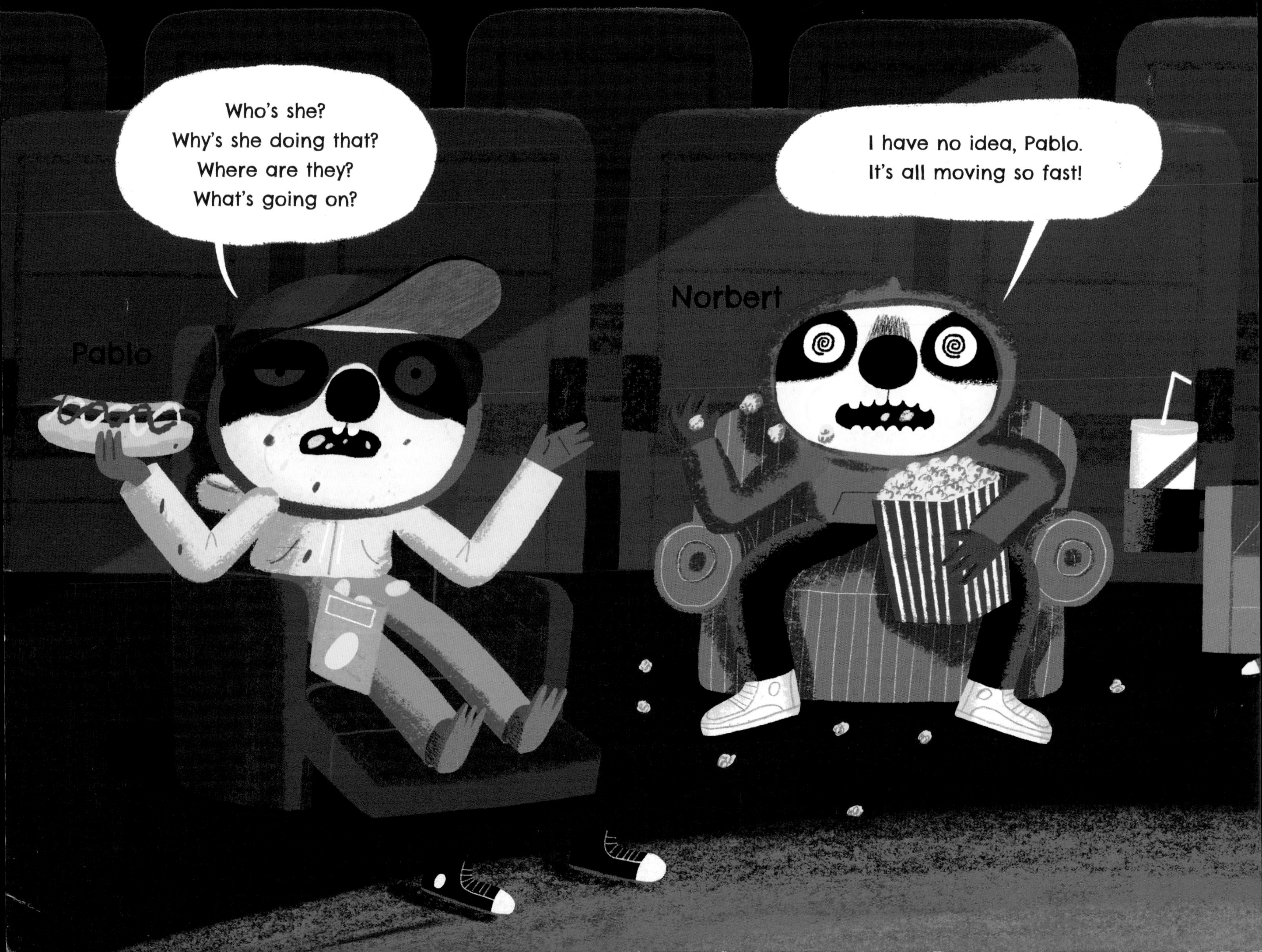

Would **YOU**
like to ride on
a rollercoaster?

Tilly

Ride the
rollercoaster, they
said. It'll be fun,
they said.

Brian

Samia

Which sloth would you choose to read you a bedtime story?

The suspense is killing me!

Tian Mei

Morgan

SLOTH IN BOOTS

THE VERY HUNGRY SLOTH

HOW TO TRAIN YOUR SLOTH

JAMES AND THE GIANT SLOTH

Aaaaand you'll find out what happens this time next year.
Vicky
Gabriella
What's **your** favourite bedtime story?
Gregory

What a magnificent sloth squad!
Just one question remains.

Who do the sloths choose
to be their best friend?

They
choose
YOU!

Did you know . . . ?

Sloths spend ninety per cent of their lives hanging around upside down.

When we do move, we're slower than any other mammal on the planet. Even our name means 'lazy'.

Miriam

Rianna

Being slow is actually a winning survival strategy. We don't use a lot of energy so we don't have to eat as much.

We sleep for up to twenty hours a day . . . right, I'm going back to bed.

We love to swim! We can move three times as quickly through water and can hold our breath for forty minutes.

Bear

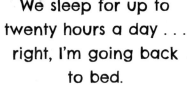

Amelie

Levi

We can turn our heads almost all the way around . . . 270 degrees, to be exact. Hi there.

We only make the dangerous journey down from our trees once a week, to poo.

Kiara

Aika

Sadly, some kinds of sloth are in danger of disappearing. You can help protect us!

20 October is International Sloth Day! It was created to raise awareness and help our well-being. Don't miss it (but, if you do, just celebrate late and enjoy the party!).

Brian

Our six species fit into two families: three-toed sloths and two-toed sloths.

Eric

Henrik

Our family names are *toe*-tally confusing, as we all have three toes on our back paws! You can tell which family we belong to by how many toes we have on our *front* paws.

Green algae grows on our fur. It helps camouflage us, and sometimes we eat bits of it as a little snack. Yum.

Michael

Thousands of years ago, giant sloths existed that could grow as big as elephants! They did not live in trees.

Amazingly, scientists have found that this algae could be used to fight many human diseases, including cancer.

Shannon

Kevin

Tian Mei

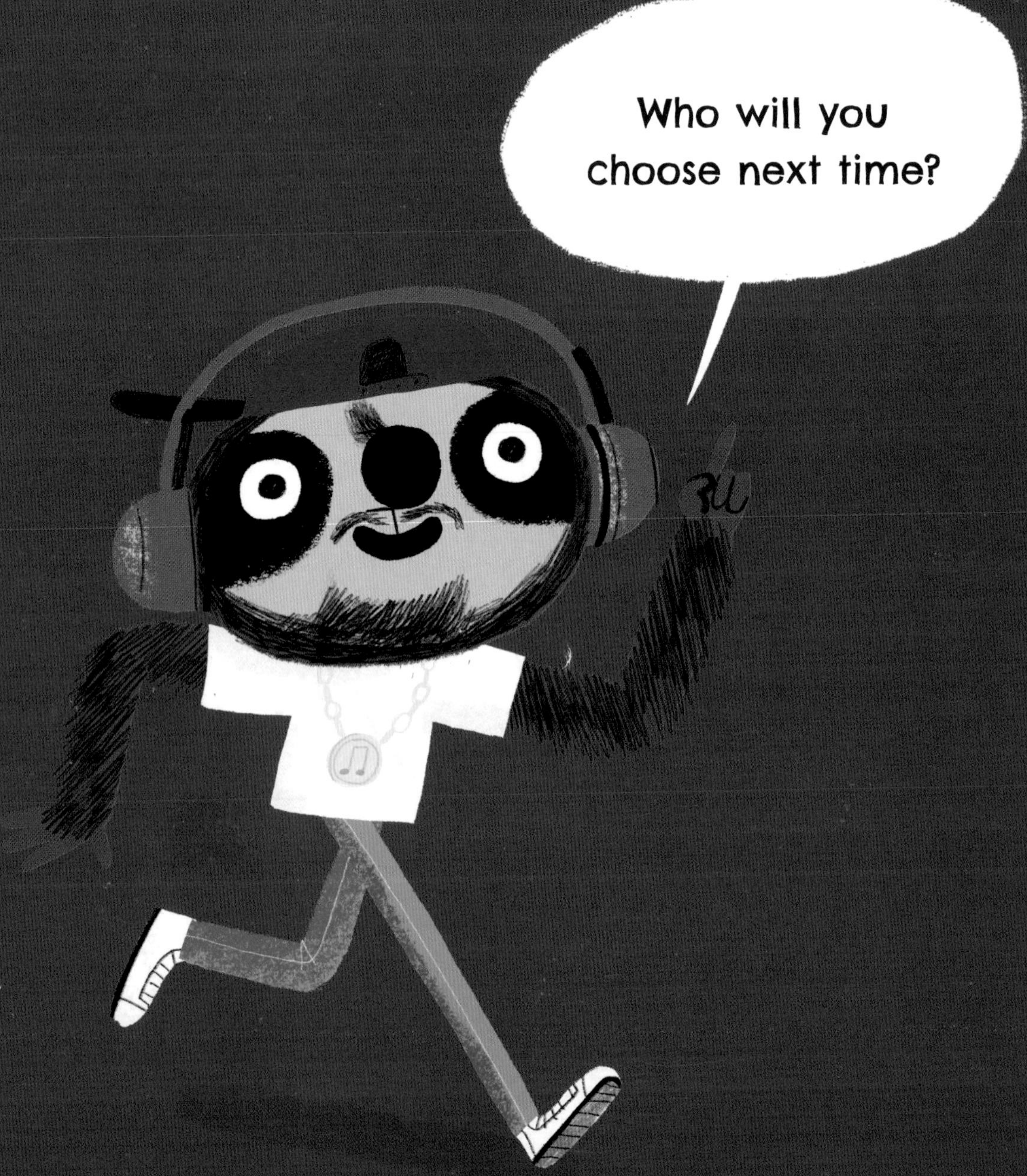
Who will you choose next time?